SUZY ORBIT, ASTRONAUT

To Bea, Rosie and Maria – superstar nieces xx
R.Q.

To A.C. and C.M.
J.T.

First published 2019 by Nosy Crow Ltd
The Crow's Nest, 14 Baden Place, Crosby Row, London SE1 1YW
www.nosycrow.com
ISBN 978 1 78800 4602 (HB) • ISBN 978 1 78800 4619 (PB)
Nosy Crow and associated logos are trademarks
and/or registered trademarks of Nosy Crow Ltd
Text © Ruth Quayle 2019 • Illustrations © Jez Tuya 2019
The right of Ruth Quayle to be identified as the author and
Jez Tuya to be identified as the illustrator has been asserted.

A CIP catalogue record for this book is available from the British Library.
Printed in China. Papers used by Nosy Crow are made from wood grown in sustainable forests.
10 9 8 7 6 5 4 3 2 1 (HB) • 10 9 8 7 6 5 4 3 2 1 (PB)

SUZY ORBIT, ASTRONAUT

Ruth Quayle • Jez Tuya

nosy crow

Suzy Orbit was a space engineer.

She lived with her boss, Captain Gizmo, in a space station on a dusty corner of the moon.

One starry morning, Suzy Orbit was busy fixing the control system when . . .

BEEP! BEEP! Captain Gizmo received a phone call from Earth.

"Aliens have been spotted in the solar system. Prepare to launch your space pod IMMEDIATELY!"

EARTH

Captain Gizmo turned pale. "Do we have a space pod?" he asked.

"Not exactly," said Suzy Orbit, "but I do have a lunar lander and an old bike. I'll **make** a space pod!"

"That's **not** a good plan," said Captain Gizmo. "It won't be **fast** enough! I'll order one right now!"

Captain Gizmo flicked through his favourite catalogue and chose a shiny new space pod.

But when the shiny new space pod arrived . . .

. . . it would **not** work because Captain Gizmo
did not have the right batteries.

"Uh-oh!" said Suzy Orbit.

Captain Gizmo was **still** hunting for some batteries when –
BEEP! BEEP! – there was **another** phone call from Earth.

ALIENS ARRIVE
00 11 07
HOURS MINUTES SECONDS

"Aliens are approaching the moon. Get dressed in your smartest spacesuit WITHOUT DELAY!"

Captain Gizmo rushed
to find Suzy Orbit . . .

"Do we have a shiny new spacesuit?" he asked. "Not exactly," said Suzy Orbit, "but I do have Aunt Edna's silver cardigan and some intergalactic goggles. I could **make** a spacesuit!"

"That's **not** a good plan!" said Captain Gizmo. "It won't be **smart** enough! I'll order one right now!"

Captain Gizmo searched on 47 websites and finally clicked on a shiny new spacesuit.

But when the shiny new spacesuit arrived . . .

it was four sizes too small.

"Uh-oh!" said Suzy Orbit.

Captain Gizmo was just sending the spacesuit back when –
BEEP! BEEP! – Earth was on the phone **again**.

Captain Gizmo raced over to Suzy Orbit.
"But I don't speak Alienish!" he gasped. "Do we have
a speak-o-phone that will translate everything I say?"

"Not exactly," she said, "but I have lots of useful stuff
in the workshop – I can definitely **make** one!"

"That's **not** a good plan!" cried Captain Gizmo.
"We can't have stuff made from old junk!
I'll order one **right now!**"

But the Intergalactic Phone Shop had run out of speak-o-phones.

The next delivery was not for **two whole weeks.**

Captain Gizmo was still sobbing when –

DING

DONG

– the doorbell rang.

It was the aliens!

"Do not panic," said the chief alien through his speak-o-phone.

"We are friendly aliens. We come in peace."

"Phew!" said Captain Gizmo.

"What good news!"

"Um, there is also bad news," said the chief alien. "A meteoroid storm is about to blast Earth and you have two minutes to stop it. Good luck!"

And then the aliens left.

"SUZY ORBIT!" wailed Captain Gizmo.
"Do we have a top-of-the-range meteoroid blaster?"

"Well," said Suzy Orbit, "not exactly."
"It's all over!" Captain Gizmo wept. "We're doomed!"

"But," said Suzy Orbit . . .

"we do have . . .

Captain Gizmo gasped. "When did you order that?"

"I didn't order it," said Suzy Orbit, smiling. "I **made** it."

Captain Gizmo's eyes lit up like stars. "It's **exactly** what we need," he said.

Suzy Orbit and Captain Gizmo strapped themselves in.

And with Suzy at the controls,
they blasted into the meteoroid storm.

They dipped and dived. They made perfect loop-the-loops.

And they shot each of the meteoroids all the way back to the darkest depths of the solar system.

Then they flew safely back to their dusty corner of the moon.

"Does your marvellous machine have a name?" asked Captain Gizmo.

Suzy Orbit smiled. "Not yet," she said, "but let's call it the Super Suzy Blast-O-Matic."

"Good plan!" said Captain Gizmo. "We don't need to order anything ever again."

"Well," said Suzy Orbit, "nothing except . . .

SUZY'S ROCKET SHIP

by: Suzy Orbit

shuttle fin

rocket nozzle

turbine

rocket booster

glider wing

hyper-thrust rocket booster

scooter wheel